stories from india

under the banyan

Eyes on the Peacock's Tail *a folktale from Rajasthan*
Magic Vessels *a folktale from Tamilnadu*
Hiss, Don't Bite! *a folktale from Bengal*
A Curly Tale *a folktale from Bihar*
All Free *a folktale from Gujarat*
Mazzoo Mazzoo *a folktale from Kashmir*
Wrestling Mania *a folktale from Punjab*
Sweet and Salty *a folktale from Andhra Pradesh*

© & ℗ 2002 Karadi Tales Company Pvt. Ltd.

Mazzoo Mazzoo (English)
ISBN 81-86838-74-0
First reprint, 2005

Produced by
Karadi Tales Company Pvt. Ltd.,
PO Box 8732, Adyar, Chennai 600 020, India
phone 91 44 4421775 *fax* 91 44 4422443 *email* karadi2000@vsnl.com

Book produced by
Tulika Publishers, 13 Prithvi Avenue, Abhiramapuram, Chennai 600 018, India
email tulikabooks@vsnl.com
website www.tulikabooks.com

Printed and bound by
APR Brothers, 159 St Mary's Road, Abhiramapuram, Chennai 600 018, India

For more information about Tulika or to order books visit our website.

www.tulikabooks.com

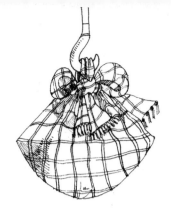

Tulika

a folktale from kashmir
Mazzoo Mazzoo

by Sandhya Rao
art by Srividya Natarajan

N azneen! Nazneen!" Maqbool Butt called to his wife as he stepped into the house.

Nazneen came rushing to greet him, her long silver earrings jingle-jangling. "I was putting the children to bed," she said. "You're really very late today! I was getting worried."

The children heard their father come in. They rubbed their eyes awake and hurled themselves at him.

"Aaah!" said Maqbool as he picked up Fahima and kissed her.

"Ooof!" said Firdaus as his father picked him up and gave him a kiss. "Your beard tickles!"

"Sorry! Sorry! Maaf kariv!" he said to his wife. "I know I'm late, but look! See what I've brought!"

Fahima, Firdaus and Nazneen waited eagerly as Maqbool fished out from the folds of his thick, long, dark blue pheran, a medium-sized newspaper package. Carefully he undid the string and opened it out.

"Wah!" said Nazneen, clapping her hands. "How did you know I wanted to make marz . . .?"

"Let me see, let me see!" cut in Fahima as she scrambled to take a peek.

"Make what, Ma? Make what?" wailed Firdaus. He craned his neck but he was really a very little fellow. Nazneen held the package low so both children could see what lay inside — large, round brinjals, purple streaked with white, fresh and squeaky smooth.

The next morning was bright and sunny. As usual, Fahima and Firdaus ate up their breakfast of fresh, home-baked bread dipped in noonchai, salted tea, from the samovar. "Quick, Fahima!" called Firdaus. "Jal jal yi!"

"Coming!" Fahima yelled back and ran to catch up with Firdaus and their friends.

Maqbool too straightened the cap on his head and set off. "I won't be late today," he promised with a smile. After all, there was a lovely dinner to look forward to.

"Inshallah!" said Nazneen. She stood by the door and watched them all go down to the Nagin lake. Their little wooden house overlooked the lake. The lofty chinar trees — the Banyan of Kashmir — looked down benevolently and ripples of water glinted in the sun. They seemed to be laughing at the antics of the fluffy white clouds in the blue, blue sky. The lake was full of shikaras, brightly decorated houseboats, all waiting for the tourists to arrive.

By late afternoon the tourists had all arrived on the lake. The air was filled with the sounds of water slap-slapping against the boats, squeals of sudden laughter and bits of conversation floating around. All the sound from inside the house was an occasional clang of pots and pans, and the gush of water from a tap. Nazneen was busy in the kitchen. She was cooking something really special — marzwangan kurma, a delicious Kashmiri dish traditionally made with tender brinjals.

"Oh, we haven't eaten marzwangan kurma in years!" said Nazneen to herself. "Come to think of it, the children haven't ever had it before!"

And she set to work as she hummed a lilting folk tune.

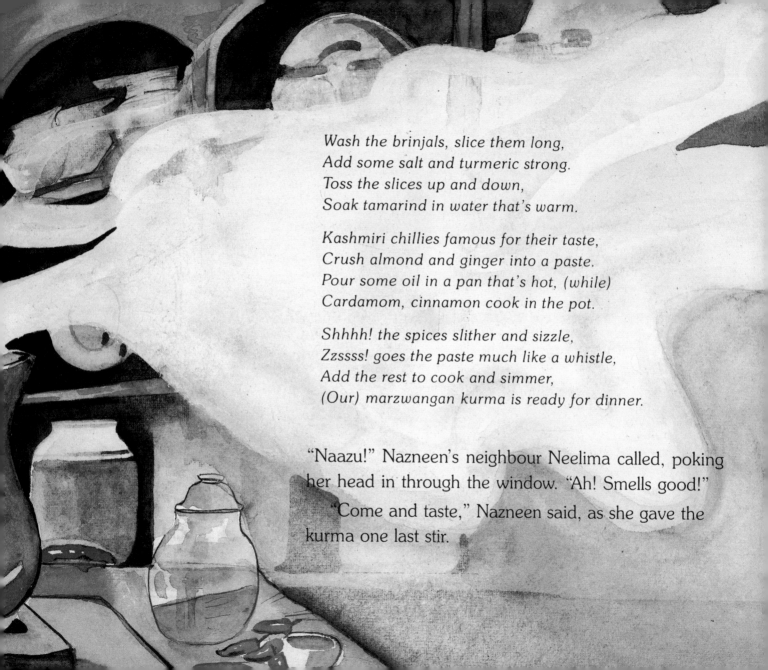

Wash the brinjals, slice them long,
Add some salt and turmeric strong.
Toss the slices up and down,
Soak tamarind in water that's warm.

Kashmiri chillies famous for their taste,
Crush almond and ginger into a paste.
Pour some oil in a pan that's hot, (while)
Cardamom, cinnamon cook in the pot.

Shhhh! the spices slither and sizzle,
Zzssss! goes the paste much like a whistle,
Add the rest to cook and simmer,
(Our) marzwangan kurma is ready for dinner.

"Naazu!" Nazneen's neighbour Neelima called, poking her head in through the window. "Ah! Smells good!"

"Come and taste," Nazneen said, as she gave the kurma one last stir.

It was evening. "The children should be back any time now," Nazneen said as she peered down the road. Then, as she turned to take the clothes off the line, she saw two men come up from the lake. It looked like . . .

"Shabbir Ali and Javed Khan!" Nazneen exclaimed. Oh no! She certainly didn't want them visiting at this time. They waved when they saw her. "If these two come home now, they will sit and sit and simply not leave."

Quickly she dashed into the house, grabbed the pan of marzwangan kurma — it was still warm — tied it up in a thick cloth and hung it from a beam near the ceiling. She had barely got off the stool when a voice said in greeting: "Varay chhak? How are you?" It was Shabbir Ali.

"We were passing and thought we'd drop by," said Javed Khan.

"Oh, I know why you're here," thought Nazneen, although she smiled. "You just want a free dinner. But you won't get it, not if I can help it."

"My husband said he would be late today," said Nazneen. "He had a lot of work at the office."

"Never mind, we'll wait," said Javed.

Just then, the children burst into the house.

"What's that lovely smell, Ammi?" asked Firdaus.

"Abbujaan said he'd be back early," said Fahima. "Has he come?"

"Say hello to Javed Bhai and Shabbir Bhai," replied Nazneen. "I was just telling them that Abba will be late." She winked at the children. But they paid no attention!

"No, Ammi, he said he would come early," said Firdaus.

"Not late," added Fahima. Nazneen looked quite helpless.

By the time the children had washed up, Shabbir and Javed were drinking their seventh cup of noonchai. They had polished off two plates full of small, hard, home-made buns, and now were munching their way through a plate full of laddoos. And yes, they didn't look like they were going anywhere in a hurry.

"Begum, that smells wonderful," came Maqbool's voice as he came into the house. Then he saw his visitors and stopped short.

"Oh good, you're back," said Javed.

"Now we might as well have dinner with you," said Shabbir.

Both Nazneen and Maqbool enjoyed having friends over for a meal. But uninvited guests like these . . . that was different!

"Well . . . yes . . . you see we would love to have you but there's not enough marz . . ." Before he could complete the sentence, Nazneen started to cough.

Seeing his mother cough, Firdaus imitated her. Cough! Cough! he went.

But Javed and Shabbir had understood the family's dinner plans. Hot hot rice with marzwangan kurma! Mmmm! They were not going to let go of that! Suddenly Javed started to jump up and down, up and down.

"Hey, what's the matter?" said Maqbool.

"Uncle is jumping!" shouted Firdaus. "Why is he jumping?"

"Water. Give him water," said Nazneen.

Javed began to scream and shout. The children started to cry. Maqbool and Nazneen did not know what to do. Now he was waving his head about, and now his eyes were rolling in his head. "Mazzooooo! Mazzooooo! Mazzooooo!" he buzzed like a hundred bees.

"Oh! Oh! I know what the matter is," said Shabbir.

"What?" the others screamed in chorus. Firdaus, too, in his little high-pitched voice. "What?"

"The great marzwangan spirit has entered Javed Mian! It will not leave until you give him marzwangan kurma to eat!" said Shabbir. "And yes, me too," he added.

Well, guests are guests. Nazneen took down the pan. Maqbool laid out two plates and Nazneen piled them high with rice. Then she served the kurma on top.

"Fantastic!" Javed and Shabbir exclaimed as they ate and ate and ate till there was nothing left. Then with loud burps they stretched out on the floor and fell asleep.

"They finished off everything!" Fahima complained, angry tears rolling down her cheeks.

"Khaaaaaaooooon!" Javed snored. "Ghaaaaaoooon!" Shabbir snored.

"Look at their stomachs!" said Firdaus. "Going up, coming down! Up, down! Up . . ." "Must be marzwangan spirit," Fahima said with a giggle.

Firdaus put his ear to Javed's belly. "Mazzoo Mian tickles!" he said.

Nazneen and Maqbool looked down at the two big men lying like babies on the floor. They looked at the children who were giggling helplessly and they too started to laugh.

Mazzoo! Mazzoo! Mazzoo! Mazzoo!